I0683755

The Fight of His Life

Jennifer Degenhardt

Translated by Charlotte Meyer

Cover art by Victoria Meyer

For all students figuring out who they are.

table of contents

ACKNOWLEDGEMENTS

A hearty thank you to Charlotte Meyer for the translation of this story. More so, I thank her for suggesting that this story be offered in English and for her unwavering patience with the length of time it took to complete this project. Hopefully it is well worth the wait.

Thank you, too, to Victoria Meyer for the beautiful cover art.

And thank you to A.J. Albano and Aidan Gaffney, both wrestling coaches, who inspired me in to write this story. With the opportunity to work with them, I not only learned more about the sport, but more importantly, the essential role of good coaches in the lives of teenagers.

Chapter 1
J.P.

With my backpack and my gym bag, I walk a mile to school this morning. It is autumn, and recently it started getting cold, which normally doesn't start until the end of this month. The walk to school when the weather is good doesn't bother me, especially when I'm on my skateboard. But when it's cold, the mile is a nightmare. Not only do I have to get up much earlier because it takes me twenty minutes longer to get there, but the wind is horrible. For me, it's another injustice of living in this community. The rich people live farther from the school and the district has buses for their children. It doesn't matter that the majority of those students come to school in their own cars or with their parents.

The wind hits me again when I turn on Edmonton Street. Only ten more minutes.

My backpack and gym bag are heavy. Until I came to this school, I didn´t know there could be so much homework. Every night I have to do two or three hours of homework. At the school where I used to go, the teachers were lucky if the students even came to class, so they didn´t give us homework. That school was called Buenaventura High School, but it wasn't that good and not much of an adventure. At that time, I lived with my mother, my Aunt Alma, and my cousins, Carlos, Juan, and Amelia. We lived there for ten years after my parents separated.

Just as I arrive at the entrance to school, I receive a Snapchat message on my cellphone. It's a crazy photo of my friend, Will, the captain of the wrestling team.

The photo is a selfie of Will with a goofy face. The usual. But anyway, he makes me laugh. I have trouble answering because I have to take off my gloves and I'm freezing, but I manage to write, "Of course, dude!"

In two weeks, the winter sports season will begin. This will be my first year on the wrestling team in this state. Unlike in Iowa, New Jersey, or Pennsylvania where the sport is really big and important, wrestling here isn't that big of a deal. Yes, there are schools with excellent athletes, but it's not a popular sport like football or lacrosse. It seems to me that in this state it is not as important as other sports. It's a pity because for me, as a Mexican, wrestling is the best.

Will waits for me in the lobby of the school and we go down to the locker room next to the gym to put away our uniforms. Will excitedly tells me, "This season is going to be great, don't you think? We are going to have a lot of different meets because of the change in the state conferences."

Will continues talking when we run into Mr. Waller, my English teacher.

"Hello, Mr. Waller," I say to him. "How was your weekend?"

"Hello, Juan Patricio. It was good, thank you. We need to talk about your grade in my class. When do you have some free time today?"

Oh, no! My grade in English class. That class is hard for me.

Mr. Waller and I make a plan to meet during seventh period. I know that my grade is a problem, but the work we have to do is very difficult for me. I decide to think about something else at the moment.

Without stopping, Will continues to talk. "Jacksbury has a good team with those guys in the 106, 113, 138, 152, 195, and 220 weight class, but in the other categories I think we can dominate. What do you think?"

"Yes," I tell him.
"Hey, you weren't paying attention, man."

*****

At 1:30, I enter Mr. Waller's room.
"Hello, Juan Patricio," he greets me.

Everyone calls me J.P., but this teacher insists on calling me by my full name. I hate it.
"Good afternoon, Mr. Waller," I respond.

"Juan Patricio, at the moment you have an F in my class. You are failing English."

"Yes, sir. I know that my grade is bad. But I try to complete the work the best I can. It's difficult for me because I don't read very well."

"I understand perfectly. Because of this, I want to help you. Come see me after school every day this week and we will work together."

"But, Mr. Waller, I have wrestling practice every day," I begin to complain.

"Juan Patricio, although I don't know much about school sports, I know that the season begins in about two weeks. And, as I see it, if you don't take advantage of my help and you fail the class, you aren't going to be able to participate. Isn't that right?"

Although I don't want to think about it, he's right. "Yes, sir. I'll see you at 2:30."

Mr. Waller smiled at me and said, "That'll be fine. I'm going to call your father, so he knows."

"Please, sir, don't call him. He's going to be mad at me."

Chapter 2
Juan

"J.P!" I shout upon entering the house. "J.P.!"

"I'm coming!" he responds.

In that instant I hear the "clump, clump, clump" of the footsteps of my son coming down the stairs. He has been living with me lately, for some four months, since the time I took him out of foster care in Arizona. He and his mother did not get along very well when he was growing up and since his aunt could not care for him, I had to go to Arizona to get him. Although it was a little difficult for all of us, J.P., my wife, and my daughters, I am very happy he is with me again. This situation is only one example of the difficulties we have, but the most important thing is that they have adapted very well.

"J.P." I say to him, "I received a phone call today from a Mr. Walken or Walter..."

"Mr. Waller," he corrects me.

"Yes, son. Mr. Waller. He told me you have an "F" in his class. But he also told me that he wants to help you to pass."

"Yes, Dad. I am going to have to stay after school every day so he can help me. But I am going to miss practice for wrestling."

"Son, I know that practice is important to you, but you also know that there will not be a spot on the team for you if you don't have good grades. Besides, it was for a good education that we moved to this town and why I took you out of that situation in Arizona. Although your mother and I are not together anymore, back when you were barely a year old, we decided to leave behind our life in Mexico and come to this country in order to offer you a better life than what we had."

Anxiously, my son says to me, "Yes, Dad, you've told me that story before."

"No, son. You only know a little of it. Sit down and I will tell you all of it."

So, I made my only son sit down to tell him the truth.

"When I was a boy I lived in a community in the D.F., the Federal District, the capital of Mexico. As you know, my parents did not make much money. My father worked as a mechanic and my mother stayed home to take care of my siblings and me. There were eight of us in all, three older siblings and four younger ones. My oldest brother was Tito and when he was 18 years old, he started to wrestle locally."

J.P. interrupted me. "Wrestling? Like the sport I'm doing? I didn't know it was popular in Mexico, too."

"No, son. Although it has the same name as the sport here in the Unites States, it is a sport more like WWE fighting, or Winning Wrestling Everywhere here in the United States."

"The same as I see on TV and YouTube? That has its main office in Strasburg?"

"Exactly," I explained to him. "It's more like entertainment than a sport, but there are athletic elements, also. And like the wrestlers of the WWE, the Mexican wrestlers adopt personalities, but they also wear masks to hide their identities. Let me look for some photos I have here in the desk drawer.

I am getting the photos when I hear my cell phone ring.

"Hello?" I say when I answer it.

The person who is calling me is the head of the second shift of workers of the cleaning company that I own. He tells me there is a problem with one of the trucks that they need for work.

"J.P., we'll continue talking later. Santiago has called me with a problem, and I need to drive to Jacksbury to resolve it."

"Okay, Dad. Let's talk later."

Chapter 3
J.P.

After two weeks of help from Mr. Waller, I am able to improve my grade in class enough to start official practice with the team this afternoon. I still can't believe my Uncle Tito was a professional wrestler in Mexico. What a life! Of course, the sport is completely different from what we practice in school, but I don't care. It's fascinating!

At that moment I receive a text from Will:

"Don't forget to go by the nurse's office and take that hydration test. See you at practice."
"Ok. I won't see you in English class?"
"No, my mother is picking me up because I am getting my driver's license at 10:00."
"Wow! Good luck."

Will just turned 16 a week ago. And like all the teens in this town, it's a tradition to get your license immediately. The majority of the kids have their own cars here. Will isn't one of them, nor I, but we want our licenses anyway. I imagine that Will's mother wants him to get his license so that he can drive to the wrestling matches that begin very early on Saturday mornings.

Like Will, I'm not going to have a car, but the license means I will become, in part, an adult – at least in my opinion. If the state thinks that I am responsible enough to drive, perhaps my father will think the same thing.

I won't turn 16 until the beginning March, just when we will begin preparing for the state championship. Although it's my first year at this school, one of my goals is to participate in the last competition at the state level. Well, there is a lot of work to do before March, like studying for the license test and preparing for the championship.

*****

The first practice of the season is at the same time exciting and torturous. It doesn't matter how much we think we are in shape, it's painful. My body hurts everywhere. The coaches Vera and Griffin make us do a lot of sit-ups, repetitious exercises, and finally a two-mile run. I can barely move now.

*****

Fortunately, there is very little wind this afternoon and it's quite sunny. On the way home, I think about the other part of the story that my father told me the other night. He told me that his brother was a professional wrestler, but he admitted that he was also a wrestler. That was a big surprise!

Evidently, when they were young, my father and his brother Sandro, used to accompany their older brother, Tito, to the local competitions. The two boys carried their big brother's gym bag. Their brother participated in the local competitions at that time under the name "The Golden Boy." His mask, like all the masks of the Mexican wrestlers, covered his whole head, except for the holes for his eyes. It even covered his mouth. The material was a type of nylon with made of bright gold fabric. The mask also had lines in black around the eyes to give the impression that he was very violent. He was champion of the central district in the featherweight class until he died in a car accident when he was 22 years old.

Then, when my father was 15 years old, he left school to enter the world of wrestling. He entered as a flyweight and competed for two years at the same level as his brother.

*****

Suddenly, I hear the sound of a horn. "Get out of the street, kid!" a man shouts at me from the window of his BMW. I am so distracted by my father's story that I walk right through the main intersection of Newtown and Main streets without paying attention to the signal and I am almost run over by a car.

Chapter 4
Juan

It is six-thirty in the evening. The front door slams meaning that J.P. has arrived home.

"Dad! Norma!" shouts J.P. when he enters the house. "What's for dinner? I'm dying of hunger!"

J.P. is a typical teen: he thinks about very few things, two of which are food and sports.

"Hello, J.P. Why are you shouting? Why can't you enter the house and just greet your family nicely?"

"You're right, Dad. I'm sorry. But the truth is, I am very hungry. Practice today was really hard."

My wife, Norma, enters the kitchen and says to J.P., "Go take a shower, son. We are eating in fifteen minutes."

I married Norma seven years ago. She is Hispanic also, from Venezuela. We met when we were working Leslie McKay's house. She's the president of WWE.

Dinner is *arepas* with white cheese and beans, and a salad. Norma says that the salad is her

"Americanization" of the meal, meaning that typically Venezuelans don't eat it with *arepas*, but "it's important to eat vegetables," she tells me.

Alana and Isabel, my daughters, sit down to eat; they are 5 and 6 years old. When they quiet down a little bit, I ask J.P. how his practice went. He answers me but changes the conversation to continue what we talked about the other day.

"Dad, I am fascinated that you were a wrestler. Why didn't I know about this part of the story before?"

"Well, I always tell you and your sisters that education is most important and there is nothing more essential than studying. But the truth is, I quit school when I was 15 years old."

"What? What?" say Isabel and J.P. at the same time.

"Isa and Alana, you've already finished eating, so go play in your room," says Norma.

"Let me explain a little. It's a long story."

Norma begins to clear the table and then starts to wash the pots and pans.

Just as I am about to tell him the whole story, J.P. interrupts me, as always. "You didn't graduate from high school?" he asks me.

"No, son. After all those years watching your Uncle Tito in the gym, I began to practice at home. At night, hidden behind our little house, I did exercises and practiced the movements I had seen during the competitions. One Saturday I went to a local competition with Tito and Sandro to watch the fighting. At that time, both of your uncles participated. Anyway, the main coach indicated that the man from the flyweight class didn't show up, so I offered to take his place. The rest is history."

"But, if you participated only on Saturdays, why didn't you graduate from high school?"

It surprises me that J.P. is asking me about school. "At that time," I tell him, "and throughout Mexico, there were no laws that existed requiring children to complete their education like there are in the United States."

"And it wasn't important to your parents?" J.P. asks, not believing.

"You have to understand, J.P., my parents worked so much just to feed the family and pay the bills that they had. They didn't have time to help us with things that had to do with school."

J.P. doesn't move at the table where we are seated and listens attentively – almost a miracle for him because always moves around and talks a lot. "And then what happened?" he asks me.

I continue with the story. I explain to my son that one day they invited all the local wrestlers to participate in a regional competition. We traveled about 300 kilometers (186 miles) on an old bus to a town called San Dieguito.

"There we participated in the competition. We fought well and became regional champions. Later, the program directors invited me to practice with their wrestlers."

Chapter 5
J.P.

It is a Wednesday, the day of our first high school wrestling meet. It's only a competition between two teams, our school and Westmoreland. Will tells me that the Westmoreland team typically isn't very good. Their school doesn't have many participants because the popular sports there are football and lacrosse. And just like our school, the students practice all year round. They say it increases the chances of getting scholarship if one specializes in a sport. But I ask myself, if most of them have the money to pay for a university, why do they need a scholarship?

Before going into history class, I send a text to Will:

"Are you ready for the meet today?"
"Of course! We are going to win!"

*****

The meet doesn't begin until four in the afternoon, but since I don't have a car or anywhere to go, I stay at school. I know I should do a little bit of homework, but I don't feel like it. Finally, I go down to the gym to look for Coach Griffen. He is with a group of teachers, training them.

"Hi, J.P.," he says. The teachers are sweating a lot. They are sweating too much, it seems to me.

"Hey, Griff."

"Are you ready for today?"

"Yes. Who am I wrestling against?"

"I don't know, exactly, but the two possibilities are a freshman or a junior, if he's not injured. It doesn't matter. You're going to win."

"Okay. Thanks, Griff."

Right then, I see Will as he enters the gym.

"You went home?" I ask him.

"Yes. I have a car now. It's so cool to drive by myself."

"I imagine it is."

Will asks me, "When will you turn 16?"

"In March. I spoke to my father the other night about the driving test."

"Nice. Is your father coming to the meet today?"

"Yeah. He tells me that he is coming to all of them. Do you know that he was a wrestler in Mexico when he was young?"

"What? For his school?"

"No."

I explain to Will how wrestling in Mexico is like the WWE here in the United States. For a half hour before the meet, I talk with Will about my father and his career as a wrestler.

According to my father (and Wikipedia) there are two types of wrestlers in Mexico. The *técnicos* who are "good" characters and the *rudos,* the "bad" characters. When my father quit school, he began wrestling as a flyweight and later as a bantamweight. But after two years, when he was 17, he wrestled as a featherweight until he won the national championship. He fought valiantly against the *rudos* and won the majority of his matches at the national level as a featherweight.

*****

My teammates and I arrange the wrestling mat for the competition and, before warming up and stretching, we go to the locker room to weigh ourselves. Each participant has to weigh below the weight in the class he wants to fight in that day. I weight 111.2 pounds. Perfect.

Coach Vera, arrives after work and tells us:

"Guys. Are you ready for today? It's the first opportunity you have to show what you have been practicing the last few weeks. Only you know how much effort you have made during practice and now is the time to show it. Alex, you will go first and then J.P.

Alex is a 106-pound wrestler, which is why he is going first. That gives me a little more time to get ready. Will and Andrew, the two captains of our team, step on the mat to greet the referee and the captains of the Westmoreland team. In a little while, the meet will start and so will my career as a wrestler at this school.

I put on my headphones and I go to a corner of the gym to think. I am going to have to wrestle the junior. Of course, he has experience but maybe he is still injured. I look at the mat. Alex fights well and wins the match. He has been wrestling since he was 6 years old. I look towards the door. Up until now I haven't seen my father. Where is he?

"One hundred twelve-pound class," calls the referee.

Just as I take off my headphones and go to the registration desk, I see my father. I smile.

The other boy and I start in the neutral position. I grab the arms of the Westmoreland boy and in the next move, grab his legs and throw him to the mat for two points. Although I am breathing heavily from the adrenaline, I calm myself a little and remember what I have practiced. The match continues and at the end of the first period, I am winning 5-3. The second period is similar. The two of us are strong, but in the last seconds I manage to get out from the bottom and get control, winning two points on a reverse. I am winning by four points at the end of the second period, but I want the pin to get the six points for the team. At the beginning of the third period I make a move to put him on his back. I stay there for the time necessary for the pin. After five minutes and 17 seconds, I win my first match. What a great day and a great beginning to the season.

Chapter 6
Juan

I arrive at the house with all of the equipment and J.P.'s dirty wrestling clothes and shoes. After the meet, J.P. wanted to go Chipotle with his friends. Normally I prefer that he stays at home during the week, but because he competed so well and has raised his grades which gave him the opportunity to participate, I gave him permission this time.

"Hello, Norma. Hello, girls."

My daughters start asking me where I was. When I explain to them that I was at the school for J.P.'s wrestling meet, they start pestering me with questions and comments.

"Why couldn't we go?"
"Yes, Daddy. I want to go to the school to see J.P."
"Another day," I tell them. "Norma, after dinner I am going to have to leave for work. Santiago is sick and I don't have anyone who can do his job. At the same time, too, he has to study for the naturalization exam."
"Okay, love. How exciting that Santiago is ready to take the exam finally. You are a good person

for being his sponsor so he can get his residency here in the United States."

"Thanks, Norma. But you know that without the help and support I received eight years ago, I would not be in the position I am today with the company and all."

"That's true. But you are a good person, anyway," said Norma, smiling. Then she asked me, "When you spoke to the officials at the immigration office, did you ask them about J.P.'s issues?"

"Yes, they told me that I have to talk to a lawyer and then complete some forms. Tomorrow I'll call the lawyer."

Norma answered, "Okay. Let me know how I can help you. I know how important it is to you, but especially for J.P. too, especially because he wants to get his license. Ha, ha, ha!"

"Ah, Norma. I know. I know."

Of course, J.P. is not Norma's son, rather the son of my ex-wife, but she treats him as if he were hers. Norma is a woman of strong character, but she has a big heart. Because her family lived in the Bronx with a lot of children and had little money, she became independent at a young age. She took care of the rest of the family until she left there to move to Connecticut. I met her at the residence where we both worked, she as the cleaning lady and I as a maintenance worker. At the time, I separated from J.P.'s mother when she escaped to Arizona with J.P. to live with her sister back then. Norma helped me and was a great friend. After a year, we were married.

"Ok, Norma. I have to go. Bye, kids. Sleep well."

"Okay, Juan. Take care. We'll talk later and I'll see you in the morning."

I leave the house and get in the truck. I start it and in just a few minutes I'm on the road to Jacksbury to meet the rest of the employees of my company. The work we do is clean all the Stuart's supermarkets. I started this business five years ago. The company has two different locations, one in the south and one in the north. The ones who work in the south clean the supermarket in Newell and the others, where I am going now, clean the one in Jacksbury. Without exception, all my employees are Hispanic. Just as a good person gave me the opportunity to begin a new life here in the United States, I want to offer the same to others.

Santiago has been with the company from the beginning. I met him when we worked every day on third shift for the WWE, from eleven at night until seven in the morning. Besides maintaining the facilities of the WWE in Strasburg, a building of 40,000 square feet, we cleaned the offices of the lawyers who were also located in Strasburg. Santiago is Nicaraguan, that is to say, he is from Nicaragua. He left his country fifteen years ago when he wasn't able to make enough money to support his family. He traveled through Honduras and Guatemala and then through Mexico. He told me that it was a rough trip, but he doesn't regret it because he has been able to send money to his family in Nicaragua. During the time he has been in the United States his wife has also come to live here and two or three of his five children.

With my help and the help of an excellent lawyer who helped me a while ago, Santiago is going to achieve a personal goal: to be an official and legal U.S. resident with documents. He is going to have to take the exam to become naturalized. When I took it some years ago, I remember that it had some really difficult questions like, 'Who was one of the writers of the Federalist Papers?' And, 'Who was the President of the United States during the Great Depression and World War Two?' When I studied for the exam, I asked for help from a *gringo* friend, a friend who was educated in the United States. And he didn't know the answers, either! I imagine that the majority of U.S. citizens couldn't pass that exam. But, since I wanted to get my documents, I studied the information like Santiago is doing now.

At that moment I arrive at Stuart's in Jacksbury and I see the other workers that are waiting for me so they can begin work. They smile while they chat. Although they seem happy, I see in their faces the exhaustion of being an immigrant in this country.

Chapter 7
J.P.

"Dad! Do you know where my headgear is for wrestling? I left it in my gym bag, but it's not there."

"Look for it in your room. I haven't seen it."

"J.P.?" asked Isabela, "is it orange?"

"Yes, Bela. Do you have it?"

"No. But I've seen it under my bed."

"Thanks."

I run to my sister's room and like Isabela said, the headgear is under her bed. I'm a little upset, but I don't have time to scold her because I am in a hurry. It's 7:25 and I will be twenty minutes late if I walk to school.

"Bye, Dad. Bye, Norma. Bye, girls. I have practice today until five-thirty. Will is bringing me home afterwards."

"Okay, " says my Dad. "Have a good day."

I put on my hat with our school mascot on it. It's a husky, just like the state university. It's the first of February and the cold is already here, and it feels like it's going to stay until May. I hate walking the ten blocks to school. I wish my father or Norma would take me to school like the other parents in town, but my father has to work, and Norma does, too, and besides, she has to take care of the kids. I dream of buying my own car. I will be looking for work this summer. With a car, I won't have to walk anymore. I'll have more freedom.

Even though I hate walking to school, it gives me time to think. As usual, I think about wrestling. I have a record of 32-4. The coaches, Vera and Griffen, congratulate me for my effort and for the skills I learned when I participated in karate in Arizona. My record surprises me a little, but I'm happy.

In two weeks will be the big test, the regional meet. That meet will last two days. We are going to compete Friday afternoon and all-day Saturday. If an athlete doesn't win his matches on Friday, he is eliminated and that will end his participation in the tournament. The two competitors that worry me the most are the kid from Westmoreland who has recovered fully, and the boy from Jacksbury. All of the wrestlers from Jacksbury are excellent. It seems they were born wrestling!

Just then, I receive a tweet about the regional wrestling match.

Ian Rocken
@therock

Follow

You're going down. We're gonna win the tourney.

12:00 PM - 1 Oct 2018

Man!   The tweet is from Ian Rocken, a wrestler from Jacksbury.   It has the hashtag #regionaltournament. I receive tweets all the time about wrestling, but this is the first time it's been personal. That makes me mad. Although it's really cold and I have to take off my gloves to type, I immediately write a text to Will:

"I am sending you a tweet I received."

I send it to him and wait for his reply.
In a little bit, he replies to me, "That's bad. Let's talk at school. Don't worry."

*****

At practice in the afternoon I am so angry that I almost can't concentrate. How can he attack me like that on Twitter? Although it's not the best way to solve the problem, during practice I fight hard and take revenge on my partner, Ben. After a bunch of hard and unjustified moves, Ben yelled at me, "J.P., what is your problem this afternoon?"

With all the negative energy I have in my body, I begin to yell at Ben.

"Why aren't you wrestling well today? You are weak and an idiot, too!"

At that moment all the team, along with the coaches, stop what they are doing and look at us.

Coach Griffen, asks me, "What's going on, J.P.? This behavior isn't normal for you. Come with me to the hall to talk."

I follow Griffen and we talk. I explain to him about the tweet I received this morning. Griffin explains to me that instead of getting so angry about the situation, using energy that should be saved for the tournament, I should take the high road, or in other words, not respond negatively. Griffin makes sure that I send a tweet with a confident response, but without arrogance. We talk for twenty minutes and in the end, I am feeling much better. With a slap on the head he tells me, "Okay. Enough psychologist and patient today. Go back to practice."

I enter the wrestling room and take my place on the mat with Ben. Before beginning again, I ask him to forgive me.

"Ben, I'm sorry for my bad behavior. I was frustrated by something."

Ben told me, "No problem, J.P. Let's practice."

My temper has been a problem for me for some time, and that's the reason I am living here with my father again. My mother and I didn't get along very well from the time I was ten or eleven years old. She said she couldn't control me and she moved to California, leaving me with my aunt. And when my aunt couldn't take care of me anymore, she put me "in the system" as it was called. In foster care I had even more problems. I fought a lot in school, and I ran away a lot of times from the homes where I was staying. One day my father came to Arizona to take me to live with him. It hasn't been Disneyland all the time, but with the help of a counselor, I am learning to control myself better.

After practice I walk with Will to his car. I open the Twitter app and write a reply to this guy, Rocken.

J.P. Díaz
@JayP

Follow

@therock Looking forward to seeing you @regionaltournament. Good luck to everyone.

12:00 PM - 1 Oct 2018

Chapter 8
Juan

While Norma cooks dinner for the family, I sit at the table with Isabel trying to help her with her first-grade homework, simple math.

"Daddy, I don't know the answer to this problem," Isabela says to me.

The worksheet has about ten problems that the students have to solve, but in order to create the illusion that the homework is fun, each math problem is presented in a balloon that the students can color after they complete the task.

"Isa, you know the answer. It's the same as the answer to number 6."

"Oh, yeah! Thanks, Daddy," she tells me.

Although the math that Isabela is doing is not very difficult, I like being able to help her with her homework. When I went to school many years ago, I always did well the math tests. I believe this way of thinking has helped me a little with my business. At that moment I hear the door slam. It must be J.P. coming home from practice. I don't know why, but every time he comes into the house, he has to slam the door really hard.

"Hello, family," says J. P. "I'm home."

"J.P., Come here," I tell him.

"Yeah, Dad. I'm coming," he replies.

"Hello son. Good to see you, but how many times do I have to tell you that you don't have to slam the door?"

"Sorry, Dad. But I am so excited. I have news."

I look at my son. Normally when he tells me he has news, something bad has happened at school. But this time he said he was excited. Hmmm. "What is it?" I ask him.

"Dad, you have to guess," J.P. tells me. I think about his classes, wrestling, his friends, but I can't guess. "You got a good grade on your history test?" I ask him.

"Yes, but that's not the good news," he tells me, smiling.

I try again. "Your coaches think you are going to win the tournament tomorrow?"

"Of course, Dad. But that's not news, that's an opinion," he scolds me a little.

"J.P." asks Norma, laughing, "Do you have a date with a pretty girl?"

"Norma! No! I don't have time for a social life now, I have to prepare for the tournament."

"Ok," I tell my son. "Tell me then. I have no idea what you want to share with us."

"Today during my free period, I spoke with one of the volunteers who works at the teen employment center. I mentioned that I was looking for work in the spring after wrestling ends. It turns out that she has a new store in town that is going to open the first of April and she needs a teen to help her. I talked to her for twenty minutes."

I was pleasantly surprised with J.P., not only because he was looking for work, but because he talked for a while with an adult. His attention span is a characteristic that we are trying to develop little by little. He has gone many years without receiving good direction on how to use the energy he has.

"What? You spent *how much* time talking with this woman?"

"Yes, Dad. Don't be so surprised. I talked to her about the job in general, but then we began to talk about Arizona. She has a house there in Las Cruces and I told her that I lived there with my mother for a few years."

Interesting. Normally my son doesn't talk about his life in Arizona, not with me, not with other people.

"That's good, J.P."

"But, Dad, I haven't told you all the news yet. She offered the job to me right then. I am going to begin working the day the store opens. I need to bring her a copy of my social security card and a copy of my birth certificate for the I-9 form or something like that."

Although I am very proud of my son for being so responsible and proactive, the situation also gives me a bit of panic because of the official documents. But at that moment, I don't say anything to J.P.

"Son, I am happy for you. I am so proud that you found a job and did it on your own."

"Everybody. It's time to eat!" shouts Norma from the kitchen.

Isabela drops her pencil and runs to her chair. Alana, who is watching television, doesn't move at all. She is watching her favorite show, "Dora the Explorer." J.P. enters the living room to get his little sister.

"Come on *rana*. We're gonna eat," says J. P.

Alana shouts, "J.P. I am NOT a *rana*."

Eating dinner together is the best part of the day. I love my family with all my heart. I feel complete seeing my wife, my daughters, and my son with me again.

"I also have an announcement," I mention to my family. "Today I spoke to my former boss from a few years ago, Leslie McKay. Because she is so generous, she gave me tickets to the circus that will be here next month."

The girls begin to shout. And Norma is also very happy. She knows that we don't have enough money to buy these tickets and that it is a surprise for the girls.

"She also gave me some other tickets," I say to J.P. "Her stadium in Strasberg is going to have a special event next week. It is a *Lucha Libre USA* show or, in other words, Mexican wrestling."

Now it is J.P.'s turn to be surprised. "Really, Dad? Awesome! When is it?"

"It will be on Sunday, February 7th. And after telling her that your team isn't very big, she gave me enough tickets for everyone. Tomorrow we can invite the boys to the show.

"Tomorrow?" says J.P. sarcastically. "I will text them now. And thanks, Dad."

J.P. gives me a hug, something unusual for him, and then gives one to Norma.

"Thanks for the dinner, Norma. I enjoyed it."

After dinner while Norma and I are washing the dishes, we talk about the situation with J.P. and the lack of documents. It has been a few weeks since I talked to the lawyer. He's supposed to be doing the paperwork now so that J.P. can get the documents that he needs. Norma, who is always right, tells me, "Juan, I know that you want to arrange everything for J.P. before you tell him, but it is really important that he knows the situation now. What will happen if you can't get the documents? J.P. is going to think you have lied to him all his life, right when you want to establish more trust between the two of you."

"You're right, Norma. I am going to have to tell him."

Chapter 9
J.P.

After my father's news about the event at WWE, I go up to my room to text my friends.

GUYS

> Guys, wanna go to the Lucha Libre USA show at the WWE arena in Strasberg on Sunday? My dad got tickets for all of us.

Almost immediately a long stream of answers starts arriving on my phone. All the guys answer in the affirmative.

*****

Finally, Sunday arrives, and my dad and I get ready to go. We are picking up some of the boys on the team and then we are going to Strasberg.

We arrive and park the truck. Let me clarify that: my father parks the truck. Although I have studied for the driving test a little, I still have not taken it and that's why I don't have license. But when I have it, I won't be able to take my friends with me for six months because it is the law in our state. I know a lot of teens who do it, but I know my father very well and he is strict when it comes to the law. "You are not going to go against the law," he always tells me. I don't know why he is so vigilant, but that's the way he is.

We walk into the stadium of the WWE. The building is, in a word, enormous. I look all around and it is filled with people. A lot of people are wearing shirts and ballcaps with their favorite person on them like "The Giant" and the "Flying Fly." Most of the people are Hispanic and I hear a lot of Spanish, but there are other people there too. I had no idea how popular this sport is.

Will arrives with another group of the boys and we meet them in the lobby. Ben is with him and I see that his eyes are wide open, and his jaw drops to the floor in shock. The boys all begin to talk at the same time. They can't believe what they are seeing: so many fans of this sport, or rather, this spectacle.

We enter the stadium and we look for our seats. We're very close to the ring where the wrestlers are going to perform. This afternoon we are going to see the Phoenix, the Chosen, Dragon, and Manuel the Magician. It's going to be an excellent event! Right when we find our seats, the lights of the stadium go down and the crowd goes crazy. In the spotlight, the announcer comes into the ring and begins to speak.

"Welcome, ladies and gentlemen, boys and girls. This afternoon you are going to enjoy yourselves. We have an excellent show for everyone. We are going to see a fight between the Ultimate Gladiator and the Young Warrior. The Ultimate Gladiator is now the champion of the world in the Super Lightweight Class. His opponent is the Young Warrior who was the champion in this class last year. It will be an incredible battle between the two of them. Now, sit down, relax, and enjoy yourselves. Let's gooooooooo!"

For the next thirty minutes, more or less, the two men wrestle, each one trying to be better than the other. At times, the Ultimate Gladiator has good moves and it seems that he is going to win; but there are other moments when the Warrior gains on his opponent and it is clearer that he is going to be the winner.

The boys and I are having an excellent afternoon cheering and shouting for the wrestlers, hoping that the best wrestler will win. Each wrestler has his own personality with a mask and an individual uniform. Phoenix wears a completely white mask with one red eye and the other green, the colors of the Mexican flag, the same as the colors of the tights he is wearing; while the Dragon wears a red, white, and blue mask, the same as the colors of the flag of Puerto Rico, where he was born.

In the van on the way back to town, Ben asks my father about his career as a wrestler.

"Mr. Díaz, were the wrestling competitions in Mexico the same as we saw today?"

"Yes, Ben. Almost the same. Although it wasn't as much of a production with the lights and the music. But the competitions were the same," said my dad.

Ben continued, "And have you participated in wrestling events here in the United States, or only in Mexico?"

"Well, it was because of wrestling that I came to this country. A promoter of Mrs. McKay's company came to a national competition one time in the capital of Mexico. He was looking for talent to participate in a Mexican wrestling tour here in the United States. I came here to wrestle with this company and I stayed."

Since we study Hispanic immigration in social studies class, Ben asks exactly how my dad came.

"Did you come with a work visa?" asks Ben.
"Yes.   And then I stayed here when it expired."

I am speechless. Never in my life has he told me why or how he has come to the United States. I have so many questions, but I don't want to ask my father about them until we are alone.

Chapter 10
Juan

We take the boys on the team to their homes, and now J.P. and I are alone in the truck. J.P. has been quiet since Ben asked me the question about wrestling here in the United States. It is rare when he doesn't talk.

"J.P., are you all right? You haven't said anything. That's not normal for you," I ask my son.

"Yes, Dad. I liked it a lot. Thanks, " says J.P.

"Do you remember when Phoenix grabbed Dragon's arm so hard that it seemed like he was going to break it?" I asked.

"Yes," he said in a monosyllable.

I don't know what is going on with J.P. He seemed to have fun with his friends. He cheered a lot.

"J.P., are you feeling okay?" I ask him.

"Yes, of course," answers J. P.

"Then what's going on? "

"Well, I'm confused. Why have you never told me how you came to this country?" asks J. P. with a pained voice.

"Oh, J.P. It's a long story. I haven't told you because I didn't want to admit that I broke the law

45

and stayed in this country after my visa expired. At the same time, I am a bit of a hypocrite because I always tell you that you need to follow the law."

"That's true. You are always angry with me when I tell you I am skateboarding in the street! Ha, ha! But how did my mother and I come to this country if you were already here?" J. P. asks me.

"That's a good question. Before the attacks on September 11th, the laws in the United States were not as strict as they are now. At that time, I spoke with your mother by telephone a lot and we decided that I would remain in the United States to work and then I would send her enough money to pay a *coyote* to take you through the desert."

"What? What is a *coyote*? "

"A person who helps people cross the border into the United States."

J.P. Is left with his mouth open. "You mean to tell me that my mother and I entered this country illegally? I don't believe it."

"It's true. I sent a great deal of money to your mother and she hired a person to help you. After a two-week long trip, you two arrived here."

"But Dad, we learned in class that the illegals that cross the desert in Arizona and New Mexico have a lot of problems and sometimes are tortured by gangs."

"Yes, son. You were very lucky."

Once again, J.P. is quiet. I imagine that he is thinking about how he arrived in this country. I hope he doesn't think about it too much, or at least not until I have an answer from the immigration office.

I break the silence, "J.P., next Monday you are going to be late for school. I want you to come with us to Santiago's naturalization ceremony.

My son doesn't answer me. He only looks at me with questioning eyes.

Chapter 11
J.P.

There are only two weeks until the regional tournament. Wrestling practices have been difficult. We want to be prepared for all of the opponents we will face. I know that I am going to have to fight against that guy from Jacksbury again, the same one that challenged me on Twitter a month ago. It will be an incredible match.

I meet up with Will and Ben in the cafeteria during fourth period. Will didn't see me in English class and asked me where I had been.

"J.P., where were you this morning? I didn't see you in English class."

"Yeah, I know. I was in court in Jacksbury."

Surprised, Will asks me, "What? What happened? Are you in trouble with the law?"

With a smile, I respond, "No. I went with my family to be a witness at a naturalization ceremony for Santiago, one of my dad's employees."

"Oh, really? So, now this man has permission to be a permanent resident?"

"No, man. That permission is when a person has residency, or in other words, has legal permission to live in the United States."

"Then what is naturalization?"

Although it surprises me that Will doesn't know this information, I don't want him to be ignorant like the majority of the teens at our school, so I explain it to him.

"When a person wants to be naturalized that means he wants to be a citizen of this country."

Will, always one with questions, asks me another, "And the person only has to participate in a ceremony?"

"No, my father had to sponsor him. That means that my father helped him with the process, proving that Santiago had a job, etc. Furthermore, Santiago had to take a test to show that he is dedicated to becoming a citizen. And the questions on the test are extremely difficult!

"I am really impressed. How was the ceremony?" Will asks me.

I tell him all about the experience in court, what the judge said, how Santiago recited the Pledge of Allegiance, and how at the end he applied for his United States passport and registered to vote. I also mentioned to Will the variety of ethnicities that I saw in court pledging allegiance to the flag of the United States.

"So many people want to be citizens of this country. We are lucky to have been born here."

Ben, sitting at the table with us, agreed. "Yeah, J.P. You're right."

After a few minutes we change the subject of the conversation to something a little less serious, but which has a lot of importance in the lives of 16-year-olds: the driver's license.

Will, again with the questions, "J.P., when can you get your license?"

"Will, why are you always bothering me, man? I already told you I don't turn 16 until the first week in March. But I have been studying for the exam since December."

"Then I have some questions for you," Will says to me.

"What a surprise, Will! You with the questions! Ha, ha!"

"Ok, ok. But here you have a question from the driving test: What do you do when you hear the siren from an emergency vehicle?"

"Easy," I tell him. "You have to move the car over to the right and stop."

"Very good," Will tells me. "Another one: When driving at night and you don't see any vehicles coming from the opposite direction, what kind of lights should you have on?"

This question made me think. But at the moment that I want to give him an answer, I see a Twitter notification on the screen on my phone. Since I check my phone constantly, I open the message. Immediately it makes me mad.

Ian Rocken
@therock

Follow

@JayP No way you're winning the tourney. I'll teach you who's boss. #jacksburywrestling #regionaltournament

12:00 PM - 1 Oct 2018

I show it to Will, and it makes him mad, too. "J.P., you have to give it to him in your response. It's not right that he says these things."

I respond without thinking:

Fortunately, the bell rings to indicate the start of the next period. Although I am bothered by the tweet I receive, I am also excited for the competition that is coming in two weeks. While I walk to my class, I hope that my phone vibrates again with another message from that Rocken guy, but nothing happens.

Chapter 12
Juan

WHAM! I hear the door slamming and then the footsteps of my son who's just getting home from school. "What's going on?" I ask myself.

I call to him to find out. "J.P., are you all right? Why did you slam the door?"

"Leave me alone, Dad."

"Son, what's wrong?"

"Nothing. Get out of my room."

I look at J.P. and raise my eyebrow. "Excuse me? What did you say?"

"I'm sorry, Dad. I have some issues concerning the regional tournament in two weeks, but I don't want to talk about that right now."

"All right. But tell me something. Are you having problems with the school, say, with the administration?" I ask him.

"No, no. Nothing like that. Just trash talk on social media."

"Ok. Are you hungry? Norma and your sisters are not here tonight for dinner, so you and I are alone. Do you want pizza?'

"Yes. With extra cheese."

While we wait for the pizza to arrive, J.P. and I begin to talk about one of his favorite things: my past.

And here come the questions: "How did you get here?" and "When did you quit wrestling?" and "How did your wrestling career end?"

"Oh, J.P., so many questions! Ok, listen up. I will tell you the story again."

The pizza arrives and J.P. and I sit down at the table. I explain to my son again how an agent from the WWE noticed my ability at a Mexican wrestling match in Arizona and asked me to join their company based in Strasberg. That agent paid my fare to New York, and I began to train with the other WWE wrestlers.

"And Dad did you earn a lot of money?"

"Yes, I earned a little. But you have to know that WWE wrestling is completely different from Mexican wrestling. The WWE is more like a show, that is, the wrestlers are more like actors.

"But it seems real," J.P. tells me.

"Yes, it is a trick. You have to convince the public."

I continue the explanation of the differences between the two methods of wrestling, the personalities, the classes of wrestling, and much more.

J.P. asks me, "And what finally happened? In other words, when did you stop wrestling?"

"I hurt myself one night and I couldn't continue wrestling. Another wrestler threw me to the floor really hard and I broke my back. I always wanted to return to the ring to wrestle again, but when I was in the hospital, I thought about you, your mother, and how I wasn't not going to be able to give you a better life if I couldn't work.

"Is that when you started the cleaning company?"

"Yes and no. I was very lucky to have met Mrs. McKay, the president of WWE while wrestling for her. We got along very well. She liked me. One day she visited me in the hospital and offered to sponsor me so I could become a U.S. citizen. I worked for her doing cleaning, first for the offices of the WWE building and later in her home. In reality, she gave me the American Dream."

"The American Dream. We talk about that in Spanish class. My teacher says that it doesn't exist or that it is an illusion that is put in front of people that come to this country," says J.P.

"Perhaps your teacher is right. But the truth for me is that without the help of Mrs. McKay, there is no way I would have been able to have what I have today: a successful company that provides for my family and provides work for many Hispanics in situations similar to mine many years ago."

"Well, Dad. Thanks for explaining it to me again. I am sorry for slamming the door. Now I'm going to my room to do my homework."

"Good, J.P. And you are welcome."

After cleaning the kitchen, I sit down again at the table with the mail that arrived that day. I notice immediately an envelope with a return address that says: IMMIGRATION AND CUSTOMS ENFORCEMENT. I open it and begin to read:

U.S. Immigration and Customs Enforcement

500 12th Street, S.W., Stop 5009, Washington, D.C. 20536-5009

28 January 2014

Dear Mr. Diaz,

This office received your petition for citizenship on 3 December. You are still lacking some documents. Please send them so we can process your application.

___ A registered copy of the birth certificate
_X_ The official signature of the parents on Form INS-73 (incl.)
___ A photo of the applicant

As soon as we receive the checked documents, we will process the application.

Sincerely,

John K. Pedersen

John K. Pedersen
Director of Applications
Department of ICE

I can't even imagine my bad luck. I sent all the paperwork to the government two months ago and just now they are informing me that they need the signatures of two parents, even though J.P.'s mother no longer has custody. What can I do? I haven't talked with her in a long time, nor do I even know where she is. How am I going to contact her to send her the form? And even more importantly, how am I going to convince here that it is imperative that she get her signature notarized? I only have a

month before J.P.'s birthday when he wants to get
his driver's license.

Chapter 13
J.P.

The Tuesday before the regional tournament I receive a text from Mrs. Silver, the woman I am going to work for in a month.

> **Ms. Silver**
>
> Hello, J.P. See you in a month when the store opens. I just need copies of your documents. You can send them to me by email. arenayagua@gmail.com

Although I don't have the copies, I respond to her:

> **Ms. Silver**
>
> Hi. Ms. Silver. I am going to talk to my father again tonight. If I can't send them to you by email, I will come by the store with the copies.

She answers me with the word "thanks" and an emoji with a smile. Why do adults use emojis when it isn't necessary? Weird.

Just as I was going to text my father to ask him about my documents, my phone explodes again with tweets from the Jacksbury wrestlers:

It makes me angry, of course, but the truth is, that I need to talk to my father. I call him on the phone, not only to ask him about the documents, but also to listen to his voice. He knows how to calm me like no other person.

"Hey, Dad."

"Hi, J.P. What's going on?"

"I need to send the documents to my new boss. Can you tell me where they are?"

"Uh, J.P.…. I need to find them. Can you wait until I get home from work tonight?

"All right."

"Anything else?"

"No. Thanks, Dad. We'll talk when you get home."

*****

In three days, I will have the fight of my life. I have been wrestling really well lately. I have a record of 34-2-0. I've won 34 matches since the beginning of the season. The only two matches I lost were against that Rocken guy and another guy from a school in New York in a big regional invitational tournament.

It's been a year with a lot of challenges for me. I started a new school, I had to make new friends, and at the same time I had to study a lot more. School is really difficult in this state and even more difficult in this community because the culture of the town dictates the everyone is going to attend "the best colleges." The academic part still causes me problems because Mr. Waller told me today that I did do well on the last essay. Ay, ay, ay!

My father comes home at six-thirty. Immediately I ask him about the documents.

"Dad, I need those documents. Do you know where they are?"

"J.P.! Really? The moment I get home? Give me a minute. Or five."

"Ok. Ok! But you told me that you have them and since I need them...."

"JAY P.!" my father yells at me, but really loud. "Enough, already. I need to think."

I shout at him, too. "Ok. Don't yell at me. What's going on?"

I go right to my room. What's the matter with my dad? He never talks to me in such a loud voice. Right when I'm going to start my homework, I hear my dad's voice at the door.

"J.P., can I come in?"
"Yeah."

My father enters. He is not smiling, and his eyes are sad.

"Come here. Sit down, J.P. I need to talk with you."

I sit next to my dad on my bed and listen to him when he gives me absolutely horrible news.

"J.P., first, forgive me for having yelled at you. I have to tell you something that relates to those documents that you need for work." I listen with attention. He always talks to me, but this is the first time he has talked to me with such a serious tone. My father continues:

"J.P. I can't give you those documents that you need: the birth certificate nor the social security card. The truth is, I don't have them."

"What? I don't understand," I say to my father.

"J.P. I don't have those documents because you are not a U.S. citizen."

I am left without words and with my mouth hung open, a strange situation for me. I have lived in this country since I was 2 years old. How is it that I am not a U.S. citizen? I have a lot of questions for my father, but no words leave my mouth. My whole life has been a lie.

My father continues talking and explains, but I don't listen to him. I think of the last 13 years of my life. The schools I have attended, the states I have lived in. I was there, but I wasn't. I was undocumented. I am exactly like the immigrants that we learned about in Spanish class. But I am worse because I have been acting as a citizen.

My father says to me, "J.P., did you hear? I am trying to arrange everything so that it will be ready for your birthday because I know that you want to get your driver's license."

"Dad. Thanks for telling me. But the truth is that I need to be alone right now."

"All right, J.P. I hope that everything will be okay after talking with the lawyer. You know that I love you a lot."

My father comes close and gives me a big hug. I know that he loves me, but I don't know what to think. I am really confused.

*****

The next two days before the regional tournament are very difficult for me. I can't focus during the practices with my team, I don't do my homework, and as a result, I don't pass two tests. Mentally I am not prepared for the tournament, and I don't make the effort to respond to all those tweets from the Jacksbury team. It's clear that they don't have any problems like I have. I feel alone. I probably should to talk with my father or someone else, but I don't know what I should say.

Finally, the day of the tournament arrives. Although I am not completely with my teammates in spirit, I do my best to advance to the next rounds. The first matches are really easy. Most of my team is together in the gymnasium chatting and passing time, but I prefer to be alone. I am sitting with my headphones in the corner of the gym watching the matches on the three mats and observing the other athletes and how they prepare for their matches. Some are like Will and Ben, entertaining themselves with others while waiting for their matches, but the serious athletes are isolated from the action, listening to music and I imagine, preparing themselves. I love watching it all.

Suddenly I see a group of wrestlers from the Jacksbury team. I don't know if they are coming over to provoke me or what, but I don't want to know. When they walk by, they make fun of me.

"There he is. Look."

"That's the one who's going to lose."

"He's weak."

"Rocken for the win."

I want to respond. I want to attack them with words and with punches, but this year I learned to control my temper. I don't want any problems. Not now, and especially not before the most important match of my life.

I hear my name. Rocken and I are "in the hole" for wrestling on mat number 2. It's the semi-finals. In other words, if I win the match, I can advance to the finals much later in the day. And if I win that match, I will win the tournament in my weight class. I think about all that has happened this week with the Twitter war and the lack of documents, not only for work and for getting my license, but of the lie that has been my life up until now. I'm really tired. But I don't want all the training to be for nothing. I want to show people and myself that my life is important.

Chapter 14
Juan

"Let's go, man!" I say, talking to my van.

No, it is not useful to speak to an automobile, I know, but I feel a little better doing it. After an emergency at one of the stores, I had to stop by the lawyer's office. He called me earlier to tell me that the documents for J.P. were ready. I don´t know how, but he was able to connect me with J.P.'s mother and when she received the necessary documents for processing the application for citizenship for J.P., she signed them and sent them to me by overnight mail. I thanked her a million times by phone and text.

Now I need to get to the school where the tournament is. I want to see my son's matches, of course. I want to give him his residency documents and tell him I called the Department of Motor Vehicles to make an appointment for him to take his driver's exam.

I walk into the gym where there are tons of people. The noise is incredible. I remember the very day that we went to WWE in Strasberg to watch

Mexican wrestling. In an instant I see my son chatting with friends. He has a big smile on his face.

"J.P.!" I shout to him.

When he sees me, he smiles. "Dad. You're just now getting here?"

"Yes, son. I'm sorry....I had a prob...."

"It's okay, Dad. Thanks for coming. I have *calimax* news!"

My son makes me laugh. He learned that phrase in Mexico when I sent him to visit his cousins in August. It means "quality to the max." J.P. spent two entire weeks surfing and learning more Spanish...

"What going on, J.P.?" I ask him.

"In the last few minutes of the semi-finals, I beat that guy Rocken from Jacksbury! Entering the third period he was winning 5-3 and we started in the neutral position. In an instant I thought about everything that had happened in my life and I grabbed him around the legs to knock him to the mat. Rocken fell hard and he wasn't able to react, then I did a move to put him on his back and..."

Will interrupted, "Mr. Díaz, you should have seen it. It was incredible."

"Yeah, Dad. I don't know what happened, but I did it!" said J.P..

I hug my son. "Excellent! I'm so proud of you. When is the next match? You're in the finals, right?

"Yeah. They begin in an hour," J.P. tells me.

"All right, J.P. I am going to sit over there. And I'm not going to move because I don't want to miss another minute."

I slap J.P. on the shoulder and wish him good luck. It's fantastic how he's changed in the last six months since he came to live with us. The road for the whole family has not be easy one for anyone. But seeing my son so excited in spite of all the challenges, such as moving to a new state, attending a demanding school in a wealthy neighborhood, and, above all, knowing he is not a U.S. citizen, nor a resident of this country, I don't think I have ever been prouder in my life. Win or lose the final match, I know that in the end, J.P. is going to overcome it all. I have the documents to prove it.

*****

The final match ends almost as soon as it started. With the energy and force that J.P. had, he puts his opponent in a position that the other kid couldn't escape from. J.P. wins five points keeping him on his back. I see that the opponent is breathless and can't breathe very well. J.P. decides to capitalize on the situation and puts him on his back again. And he keeps him there for the pin and the win. When the referee hits the mat for the last time, J.P. jumps up to shake hands with his opponent. At the same time, the referee raises his arm to declare him the winner.

ABOUT THE AUTHOR

Jennifer Degenhardt taught high school Spanish for over 20 years and now teaches at the college level. She realized her own high school students, many of whom had learning challenges, acquired language best through stories, so she began to write ones that she thought would appeal to them. She has been writing ever since.

Please check out the other titles by Jen Degenhardt available on Amazon:

La chica nueva | La Nouvelle Fille |The New Girl
La chica nueva (the ancillary/workbook
volume, Kindle book, audiobook)
El jersey|The Jersey |*Le Maillot*
Quince
La mochila | The Backpack
La vida es complicada
El viaje difícil|*Un Voyage Difficile*
La niñera
La última prueba
Los tres amigos | Three Friends | *Drei Freunde* | *Les
Trois Amis*
María María: un cuento de un huracán | María María:
A Story of a Storm | Maria Maria: un histoire d'un
orage
Debido a la tormenta
La lucha de la vida | The Fight of His Life
Secretos
Como vuela la pelota

Follow Jen Degenhardt on Facebook, Instagram @jendegenhardt9, and Twitter @JenniferDegenh1 or visit the website, www.puenteslanguage.com to sign up to receive information on new releases and other events.

ABOUT THE TRANSLATOR

Charlotte Meyer has taught Spanish & Japanese and currently works with ESL students. She lived in Japan for a mission, Germany for the Army, Mexico for summer school, and has visited France and Israel on tours. When she is not working with students, Charlotte's obsession is knitting and crocheting. She and her husband have five grown children, one of whom speaks Russian.

ABOUT THE COVER ARTIST

Victoria Meyer, better known by her artist name VickyViolet, is a self-taught artist and cartoonist whose work is heavily influenced by both western and eastern art and animation styles. She continues to draw every single day. Specializing in digital art, she creates both fanart and original characters. VickyViolet can be found on various creator platforms, such as DeviantArt, Tumblr, and YouTube.